The Journey

*A Covid-19
Pandemic Story
of a Woman's
Journey to Build
Her Emotional
Strength*

Jim Morrison
& Anthony McCarley

CONTENTS

FOREWORD

For Those Who Want to Accomplish Great Things®

This book is for anyone who wants to achieve something they believe is beyond what they can achieve today. It unveils a unique framework of thinking – of structuring your growth to achieve real-life, tangible results.

We have all been taught to think in binary ways about ourselves – physical or mental. Unfortunately, that is faulty thinking. Mental tends to mean anything that goes into or goes on inside your head.

In reality, the inside of your head has two main functions. One, to obtain and utilize knowledge. Two, to process emotions.

Most people believe the road to success is all about the first function and they invest tremendously in knowledge, while ignoring the more powerful function.

As you think about the people who you know who are successful, what do you notice that makes them different? Is it what they know, or how they think?

As you think about the people you like to be around, or the best boss you've had, ask yourself, "What is it that makes them different, special?" Lots of people have gone to good schools. Lots of people can physically do the job of CEO or manager. What makes the most successful different is the management of their emotions.

How can you become one of these high-performance people? How can you learn to manage your emotions to become happier and more successful?

These are the questions this book answers.

We wrote this book in fable format so that it would not read like a text book, but you should still invest the time to study the concepts introduced in each chapter.

If you invest your time by studying this book and growing your emotional strength, you will experience exponential results in your life.

INTRODUCTION

The Journey is a story of one woman's struggle to recreate her life during the COVID-19 pandemic of 2020. The book has been written entirely during the pandemic and so We believe many readers will be able to relate to our main character Jean's struggles. Like many of us she hears about the Pandemic and at first it doesn't sound like it will impact her life. Very soon she will find out that all of the pillars of her life like her job, and her home will all be impacted. Jean then needs to make some fateful choices! Fortunately she has a strong extended family who not only help her cope with the Pandemic. She also finds one special family member will teach her how to build up her emotional strength to make a new life for herself and enable her to win through the crisis. As Jean quarantines to be with her family each day she learns more about how to build her emotional strength and her life plan. By the time quarantine is over Jean still has the challenges of the Pandemic ahead but she now has a new set of tools to manage through the crisis and to take control of her life. By reading Jean's story we hope you'll also learn how to build up your emotional strength to live your best life and do great things!

CHAPTER 1

Meet Jean!

It's New Year's Eve 2020. Jean Valjean is working at a bar in San Francisco as a bartender. She is 28, and it's been a long day and night. Around 4 AM, she goes home tired but looking forward to the New Year and what is ahead in 2020. She meets her cat, Phoebe, at the door. Jean's has long dark hair and large brown eyes and is tall with an athletic build from her Pilates workouts. She's been told by many that she has an attractive face, with her high cheekbones and dark brown skin. Since Jean got her degree in Physical Therapy, she knows the importance of fitness and does a Pilates workout five days a week. This keeps her in shape and also sets a great example for her couple of personal training clients. She has a few good girlfriends that she has kept since college, and a few friends from work; but other than those and her family, she likes to keep her relationships low-key. Her bartender job brings in good money, but it limits her social life. It also means she works most nights, so she has never had a chance to focus on her childhood dream of being a singer. On the bright side, she takes advantage of having her days free by spending time at Golden Gate Park or Ocean Beach, and she likes to work out at both.

CHAPTER 2

Meet Jean's family.

Jean grew up in Richmond, Virginia, in a tight-knit family, as the oldest of 3 girls. Her parents still live there and have been married for 32 years. As a child, Jean had a rich family life; not only with her immediate family but with her many aunts, uncles and cousins, as well as her grandparents. Jean's grandmother's parents immigrated to the U.S. from India in 1946 and started their family business in New York. They had four children; her Uncle Raghu and Aunt Amara who were born in India before they moved, Jean's Grandmother, Helen and Uncle Richard who were born in the U.S. Jean's great-grand-parents started a small Indian restaurant in Queens. After a few years, they expanded, adding an Indian grocery store and eventually another restaurant location in Brooklyn.

They believed in the American Dream, and they always felt that running your own business made you more independent. They instilled these values in all their children. Jean's Mom always told her that even though her great-grandparents worked hard, they really worked for their family and that they valued a strong personal and family life as much or more than they did their business.

As Helen and her brothers and sisters grew up and eventually left their parent's home, they stayed close. They moved to various locations on the East Coast, with Helen finally moving to Richmond. Everyone lived close enough, so there were many family events, and as is the Indian tradition, the attendees of these events included any cousins, second cousins, etc.

When Jean was growing up, her family liked to take an annual trip to see America. On one of these adventures by RV, Jean fell in love with San Francisco and the Bay Area, and that helped her decide to go to college there. She graduated from the University of San Francisco in 2008 with a B.S. in Physical Therapy. As a student, Jean had plans to become a physical therapist. But as she got closer to graduation, the thought of an extra 3 – 4 years of schooling didn't appeal to her anymore, so Jean started to think of a job that would give her some flexibility to pursue her childhood dream of being an entertainer. While she had dreams of being a singer and doing something important, she had no solid plans. That led Jean into becoming a server at a local restaurant, to enable her to pay her bills, until she eventually moved up to being a bartender, which is fun and where she gets great tips. She loves the job, and the people, and so she has stayed with it over the last few years. Jean is still hoping to get her singing career going, but it is a tough business to get started in.

Jean lives in a basement studio apartment in Pacifica, a small town just south of San Francisco. Her apartment is in the lower level of a home, and her landlord is Mrs. Chen, who lives alone above her. Jean has been in the apartment for about four years and has developed a great relationship with her landlord. She often helps her out around the house, or when something needs to be done.

CHAPTER 3

Jean attends a family celebration.

On February 2nd, 2019, Jean flies into Richmond, VA, for a family party. It's her Grandmother Helen's 65th birthday, and with all the family coming, it will be a great time to reconnect with everyone. Jean's parents, John and Kashvi, pick her up at the airport and head to the family home. As they're driving home, they ask Jean how she is doing.

Jean replies, "I'm doing great! I love my job as a bartender, I'm making good money and I'm able to save a little. I've got a great group of friends in the Bay Area. While I haven't been able to establish myself as a singer like I had hoped, I do get to sing in a local theater which is wonderful. I'm not doing physical therapy like I had planned post college, but I am working at a gym as a personal trainer a few days a week. I like the people and the one-on-one interaction. Between bartending and personal training, I have all the flexibility I need to enjoy the outdoors and the San Francisco area."

"That sounds like a great lifestyle," says Kashvi.

"We're glad you're happy in San Francisco, but we'd love it if you got to visit more often," says John.

As they arrive at the house, Jean's grandmother, Helen, is already there. Helen and Jean hug, and Helen helps Jean to unload her luggage. Helen arrived early to help prepare, even though the party is for her!

"Take your things to the basement," says Kashvi, "We've fixed it up into a nice little room for you. Just like at home in Pacifica."

Jean laughs! After unloading the luggage, everyone goes out to the patio in the backyard to catch up on family things and the plans for the party over the next few days.

After a wonderful weekend celebration with family, Monday rolls around too soon!

It's Monday morning, and Jean starts packing up to head to the airport and back to San Francisco. She hears a knock on the door to the basement, and when she answers, she sees her grandmother smiling. Jean waves her in and asks if she enjoyed the party.

"I loved the party and catching up with so many friends and family," said Helen, "I wish we got to spend more time together though. How would you feel if we spend some time catching up before you leave? I'd love to hear about your exciting life in San Francisco!"

"I don't know how exciting it is but I'd love to chat with you," said Jean," Is there a good place for us to sit?"

"I always like to relax and chat in the backyard here. Your parents did a nice job, making it feel very open and private at the same time. I know it's a bit chilly, but if we bring some hot coffee, we'll stay warm," said Helen.

"Great!" said Jean," I'll meet you there in 5 minutes."

An hour and a half later, Jean's father interrupts them and says it's time to head to the airport.

Jean looks at her watch and realizes the time. "I'd better go, Grandma. It was so wonderful talking with you. Let's keep in touch."

Helen gives her a big hug and promises that they will find the time to get together more in the future.

CHAPTER 4

Jean first reads about Covid-19.

It's March 10th, 2020, and during a slow period at work, Jean reads a news item on her phone about some virus in China. It seems like something that won't affect her life, so she does a quick scan and moves on. She also checks her Instagram to catch up with her friends and update them on her week, as well as her Facebook page, where she sees more posts from her Mother and Grandmother. They've been traveling more frequently since Grandma's retirement, and they are posting from Carlsbad Caverns in Texas. They rented an RV and drove there, keeping alive the family tradition that started when Helen and her brothers and sister were children!

CHAPTER 5

Jean's loses 2 jobs in one day!

On March 20, 2020, California's governor, Gavin Newsom announced a statewide lockdown. Jean hears about it after leaving the gym, where she had taught some personal training sessions from 6-10 AM. On the way home, she gets a call from the bar where she works, informing her that they'll be closed until the lockdown has ended and she has been furloughed indefinitely. She calls the owner of the gym she just left, to see what her status is there and he tells her that all classes are cancelled, and the gym is closed until further notice. He doesn't know for sure if he'll even be able to reopen if the lockdown goes on very long since he's been running things on a shoe-string budget and doesn't have a rainy day fund. Jean heads home to Phoebe, thinking about what she can do given she just lost both her jobs!

CHAPTER 6

Jean shelters in place.

A week later, Jean is without a job, applying for unemployment benefits online, which has proven to be extremely difficult. After hours of trying to log in and complete her application, she finally gets a confirmation that her information has been submitted. Fortunately, with the Stimulus money from the federal government and the expanded unemployment benefits until the end of July, Jean can pay her rent and bills. She'll have to find a new job before then so she can keep up with her bills in the future. Jean feels she can stay sheltered in place and even still keep up her fitness routine, but she's concerned as she reads how much the coronavirus has already spread and how many businesses have been shut down.

Meanwhile, she is staying in her apartment and having everything delivered. It's a little lonely, and Jean misses physical contact with her friends, but her social network is strong, and they've already set up some recurring Zoom meetings where they are keeping in touch.

CHAPTER 7

Jean learns her family is safe together.

Besides setting up recurring Zooms with her friends, Jean also keeps close to her family. Her Mom and Grandma finished their RV trip right before the Pandemic, so her Mom, Dad, and Grandmother are all sheltering at their home in suburban Richmond. All her brothers and sister's families are safe too, and Jean is grateful no one in her family has gotten Covid-19 so far.

Jean's parents and Grandma have been staying safe and have now been together in lockdown for two weeks so they should be virus-free. Her parents suggest that Jean come home and stay with them since they have extra space, which is great news, but also a source of great concern to Jean, who doesn't want to get them sick.

"I'm good here in my apartment but thanks for the offer," says Jean.

Jean is also concerned that it seems the government is not taking the Coronavirus as seriously in Virginia as they are in California. While Jean feels she made the right choice staying in Pacifica, she wonders what will happen as her money and unemployment benefits run out. She brings this up on her next Zoom with her friends, and they all agree that staying in Pacifica in her current apartment sounds like the right idea.

CHAPTER 8

Jean loses her home!

Jean has always had a friendly relationship with Mrs. Chen, so she is looking forward to talking to her the next time she sees her when she gets an invite to a Zoom call by none other than Mrs. Chen. Even though they live in the same house, they practice strict social distancing. Mrs. Chen starts the call by asking how Jean is doing and how her family is. Jean's been living in this apartment for four years, so they've gotten to know each other very well, and Mrs. Chen feels more like a friend than a landlord. After Jean updates Mrs. Chen on her family, she asks about how Mrs. Chen and her family are doing.

Jean knows Mrs. Chen's son and has met him a couple of times. He lives in the East Bay and owns a small restaurant, so Jean figures out that times are hard for him.

Mrs. Chen reveals that that is what she wanted to talk to Jean about. Her son has asked to move into the apartment to save money since his business had to shut down everything except for takeout. Mrs. Chen says she hates to do this to Jean, but her son is family, so she feels she must. She has to move Jean out at the end of the month, so her son can have a place to stay without rent.

Jean is stunned, speechless, very angry and upset by the shocking news. She, however, tells Mrs. Chen that she understands the reason behind her decision and will move out at the end of the month.

As she ends the Zoom call, she starts to worry. All her plans to ride the Covid-19 Pandemic out have been turned upside down. She doesn't know what she'll do with no job, and now no place to live.

She spends the rest of the day in a haze, skips her workout, and orders a pizza for dinner. The pizza makes her feel a little better, but she gets depressed when she goes to bed a few hours later.

CHAPTER 9

Jean realizes she won't be homeless.

Jean wakes up the next day, feeling down. She pushes herself to do her morning workout, which helps her to clear her head and focus on her options. Now, she has two weeks to find a new place to live, and with no job, and little savings, she wonders what landlord will even rent a place to her. After thinking long and hard about it, she decides to call her parents and see if the offer to move in with them is still on the table. She feels like a 28-year-old loser doing this, but she doesn't see another valid option.

Her parents are very angry with Mrs. Chen for putting Jean out on the street, but Jean discloses to them that even though she feels betrayed, she also understands Mrs. Chen's concern for her son.

John and Kashvi, of course, agree that the offer to live with them still stands. They are very happy to get to see more of Jean than they have in the years since she graduated from college. While Jean thinks about driving to Virginia, it doesn't seem practical especially since her car has a lot of miles on it, so she sells the car, puts her small amount of belongings in storage, and buys a plane ticket. When the day of the flight arrives, she has a moment of panic and wonders if she's making the right decision.

Is giving up her life in San Francisco worth the move? How will she maintain her contacts and friends? And how will she get a job in Richmond when it seems the economic news only keeps getting worse? She encourages herself to do it and takes a Lyft to the airport.

CHAPTER 10

Jean arrives in Richmond.

After a nearly empty flight, Jean gets to Richmond still nervous about moving back in with her parents. Her Mom is waiting for her in her car. Mom, wearing a mask, tells Jean to put her luggage in the middle row of the seats and then get in the 3rd row herself. Jean is also wearing a mask, and she is glad her Mom is taking precautionary measures.

Jean asks about how Mom and Dad have set up the house so she can be in quarantine for 14 days. Her Mom says she doesn't need to do that; she's family, and also, in Virginia, they're already talking about reopening some businesses soon. Jean has to insist that her parents give her the basement as her room (she's used to living in a basement) and that they work out ways for her to maintain quarantine for 14 days. Mom agrees, and as they ride home, they talk about how they'll live together but apart.

When they get home, Dad suggests that they don't need to be so strict. Jean's grandmother Helen steps in and takes Jean's side; they all should treat this quarantine as something important. Jean's never seen her grandmother take charge like that before, and she likes it! Within an hour with Grandma taking the lead, they worked out the details of the plan and created a safe zone in the back yard where they can meet, while each of them has their own space. They are to stay over 10 feet apart (to be safer). As Jean is unpacking in, what is now, her East Coast basement apartment, she begins to feel, for the first time in weeks, the possibility that this might work. Jean goes to sleep feeling hopeful and gets the best night's sleep she has had in a long time.

CHAPTER 11

Jean sees the opportunity to get to know her Grandmother.

As Jean gets set up in her new routine, she sees that one of the pluses of the arrangement is that she will get to know her grandmother, Helen, better as an adult than she ever did. She realizes that her memories of her are from a child's perspective, and she makes up her mind to make the most of this opportunity. As she talks with her grandmother, Jean learns that her grandmother had a remarkable life and career.

Helen grew up working in her parent's business, but after graduating from high school, she moved away from New York and her family to start her own life as an independent woman. Richmond, Virginia let her be close enough to visit and stay in touch but also far enough away to be independent. After getting married and starting a family, she started her own real estate company in the 1980s at a time when it was unusual for a woman to own her own business. Her company was very successful in the greater Richmond area, and she became known as "The Guide" for her ability to guide her clients to the perfect home. While her personal life had its ups and downs, it turned out great as well with three children and eight grandchildren. When Helen retired, she sold a thriving business to some of her associates and focused on her family and on helping others learn from her success. She stays in touch with many of her former clients and associates and does a lot of volunteer work in the community. Jean hopes that by getting to know her grandmother better, she'll learn some things that will help her have a happy and successful life.

CHAPTER 12, DAY 1 OF QUARANTINE.

Jean learns why her grandmother is known as The Guide.

Jean starts her day like she used to do at home in Pacifica, with a 50-minute workout. This physical activity always energizes her and makes her feel good. She has to adapt her routine to the equipment available in the basement, and she's able to do a new version of her Pilates routine. After the workout, she checks her phone and sees various texts and posts from her friends and family. Everyone is asking about her trip to Virginia and how she is setting up her new home. After she goes through answering their questions, Jean posts her new situation to her network of friends, family, and former co-workers. As she's checking everything online, Jean notices a friend request on Facebook from her grandmother. She accepts, of course, and begins reading her grandmother's timeline. Her grandmother, Helen, has led such a rich life and has so many friends! Jean notices that many of her grandmother's friends call her The Guide, like in her Real Estate company. Now Jean is curious about what kind of a guide her grandmother is! Jean texts her grandmother to see if she has time to talk.

They set up a time to talk in an hour so Jean can grab some breakfast and take a shower.

It's early April, and in Richmond, that can get cold, but today the weather is cool but not too cold. When Jean and her grandmother get together, they sit in the backyard in an area where the chairs are set 10 feet apart. One chair is marked 'Jean', which is the one she first reaches walking up from the basement door. The one closest to the house is marked 'The Guide', and as Jean sits down, her grandmother comes out of the house and sits in that chair. There are also two chairs set 10 feet from Jean and The Guide's chairs forming a triangle, and they are marked John and Kashvi. After exchanging pleasantries and confirming that everyone in the family is fine, Jean asks her grandmother how she got the nickname of 'The Guide'.

"Well," she says, "it just happened over time. When I started my real estate career, I used a little slogan that said, "Helen Jackson, your Guide to real estate." Then I did my best to be a guide to people when looking for or selling a home. I found that as I got to meet many different people, we often formed a bond, and to help people find the right home, I had to get to know them and what was going on in their lives. Over time my clients started asking me about real estate and other life decisions, both big and small. I guess that's natural since a home is such a big part of your life. Anyway, the next thing I knew was, when someone I'd worked with before asked me for advice, they'd call me The Guide. Over the years, I've tried to live up to the name and be the best guide I can be for all people in my life. By guiding, not telling people how to make their lives the best they can be, I believe I've helped a lot of people, and I also have found my purpose in life. Jean, I hope that as we get to know each other better, I can become your guide as well."

Jean was impressed, and realized that there was a lot more to her grandmother than she had thought. "I'd like that a lot," said Jean, "I'm feeling a little down with all the talk about the virus, losing contact with so many people, and being unemployed and homeless."

The Guide stood up and said loudly to Jean, "You are not homeless! As long as you have your family you will always have a home with people who love you. Let's keep talking every day through this quarantine and then on day 15 we will all make up for all the hugs we've missed!."

Jean realized she'd been letting her emotions get the better of her and thanked The Guide for making her realize how safe she was as part of her large loving family!

"See you tomorrow, Grandma," said Jean.

"Please call me The Guide," said Helen, I'll always be your grandmother, but for the next two weeks, let me focus on being your guide.

"OK, I'll try but I might accidentally slip from time to time." said Jean with a smile.

With that in mind, Jean and The Guide headed into the house to continue with their separate days.

CHAPTER 13, DAY 2 OF QUARANTINE

Jean begins to assess her emotions.

As Jean and The Guide walked out into their backyard the next afternoon, The Guide asked Jean how she was doing with all of the change and uncertainty in her life.

Jean thought a minute and then said she was doing fine but that she really didn't know what to do now that she lost her job and her former home so quickly. While the bartending job wasn't her dream job, it paid the rent and allowed her to live a good life. Jean said she had felt her life wasn't quite what she wanted it to be before Covid-19, but now even the good things she had are gone, except for her family and Phoebe, her cat.

"I guess maybe I'm not doing so fine after all," said Jean.

"Will you do something for me?" asked The Guide. "Jean, what I want you to do is to write down all the emotions, good and bad, you are feeling right now, and also write down your first thoughts on why you are feeling them. Then tomorrow let's talk about your list and let's see where we are and what our next steps are.

"That would be great!" says Jean. As Jean leaves to start working on documenting her emotions and why she's feeling them, she and The Guide give each other virtual hugs and head to their parts of the house.

CHAPTER 14, DAY 3 OF QUARANTINE

Jean learns the power of Identifying her emotions.

Jean and The Guide meet again in the backyard first thing the next morning. After catching up on how their days had been The Guide asks Jean if she had time to list her emotions like she asked.

"This is often one of the hardest things to do because we often don't take the time to understand what is driving the way we feel," says The Guide, "Only by understanding our true feelings and why we feel that way can we strengthen our emotional wellbeing."

"I thought about it a lot," said Jean, "There are so many things going on in my head right now it is hard to pin them down. I'm a little lost and depressed because while being here with my family is great, sometimes I feel like I went from being this self-sufficient person living her life, to being a loser who is living off my family and who doesn't have a job or a purpose. While I've thought about getting a job at a store or a warehouse that isn't my dream and I don't think it would be safe for you all either. I want to do something important that helps people and I don't see the path to get there or to even get started."

"Wow!" says The Guide, "first of all I don't want to hear you call yourself a loser ever again. All people get knocked down by life sometimes, but if you keep getting back up, you're not a loser. And you are on your feet and working through how to live the best life possible so you're on your way to being a winner. Never forget that! All that has happened to you is a lot to deal with. I think given all the change in your life and how harsh this Covid-19 environment is, you do have valid reasons for having your feelings. What we're going to do together over this quarantine is teach you how to change those feelings around so that your emotions provide you strength instead of robbing you of your strength."

"Let me tell you a story about a part of my life when I was feeling some of the emotions you're feeling," said The Guide, "A few years after I graduated from college, I found myself in a very similar situation. After graduating, I got a job in an office here in town doing customer service work. I had been working at this office job for a few years and then I got laid off and found myself kind of lost. No job, bad news in the paper and on TV every day, and no prospects of another job quickly because we were going through a recession back then. I was lucky to have a great circle of friends and one of them worked in real estate. She seemed to love her work and got to meet lots of interesting people. I didn't think I could ever be like her and I had never sold anything in my life. Over coffee one morning we started talking about it and I realized all the things she loved about her job were things I liked to do too. I still had some doubts, but she said why not give it a try since I was out of work anyway. It was very scary because I was used to getting a paycheck from my company and if I did this, I would only make money when I sold a house so all the pressure was on me!"

"How did you have the courage to make such a big decision?" asked Jean.

"Well," said The Guide, "to make this decision I had to build up my Emotional Strength and to do that I used a tool that one of my coaches taught me called Physical Knowledge Emotional (PKE). It looks like I have to go to a Zoom meeting with a friend now but let's talk more tomorrow."

Jean left their visit with so many questions and was excited to talk with The Guide again the next day! And she realized, The Guide was right; she wasn't a loser since she was still working to be a better person, and she still believed that she would do great things.

Identifying your emotions

○ **Tools:**

- Honest Self-Assessment
- Peer Review
- Active Listening

○ **Positive Trigger Words**

- Self-Awareness
- Emotional Balance

CHAPTER 15, DAY 4 OF QUARANTINE

Jean learns about Physical and Emotional Strength.

Jean gets to the backyard a little early and does some stretching exercises to loosen up. When The Guide gets there a few minutes later, Jean stops, but The Guide says, "Don't stop, I want to join you." They stretch together for another 10 minutes while catching up on their days. As they wind down the stretches, Jean asks The Guide to tell her a little about her life and their family history. While Jean has heard the stories before, she realizes that she has a new perspective on the importance of family!

"Well," says The Guide, "as you know my parents came to this country from India back in 1946. Times were hard in India after the Second World War and they wanted to start a new life. As many did, they came into the U.S. in New York and settled down in a community with a vibrant Indian culture in Queens. I think our family has always had entrepreneur blood in them and it was just so with my parents. They rented a brownstone type place where they had a small restaurant on the main floor, and we lived upstairs. My parents seemed to always be working but they always made time for us too. We all helped in the business as well as with taking care of the family and doing our schoolwork. While it seemed like the work never ended we loved our life and while we were at work we also got to be with our family! After I finished high school I worked in our restaurants and store while going to a local college at night. While it was expected that we all worked in the family business it was also my parents' belief that all of their children should go to college and get a degree. They hadn't been able to do this themselves in India, and they couldn't after they had a family but they felt this was important for us to succeed. They were so proud when I graduated with my Business degree, and so of course being an Indian-American family we had a very large family graduation celebration. Those were good times and I think I was lucky to get to learn from my parents the beliefs and perspectives that made me what I would become."

"But, let's get back to how PKE can build your emotional strength," finished The Guide.

"When you think of strength, most people talk about their physical and mental strength," said The Guide, "Physical strength is built up just like you do it. By taking care of your body and eating right and exercising like the stretches we just did. But building mental strength is more complicated. To have and maintain mental strength you need to use knowledge not only to know things like you need to know to run a business for example but you also need knowledge to strengthen your emotions. For example, I know you've been anxious and feeling depressed about your life. To turn those negative emotions into positive ones you can't just think happy thoughts, you have to have the knowledge to improve your emotions."

"I am not sure I understand how that works, but I want to know more and try to improve my emotions," said Jean, "Can you give me some examples?"

"I will," said The Guide, "Let's start with your feeling anxious because you don't have a job. First of all, let's break that down more. Are you anxious because you don't have a job or because you don't know how you'll support yourself? Those are two different things!"

"I believe I'm anxious because I don't know how I'll support myself," said Jean, "I always assumed that meant getting a job. Doesn't it?"

"Not at all," said The Guide, "supporting yourself can mean getting a job or it can also mean being your own boss and working for yourself. While working for yourself can be very hard, it can also be very rewarding. While there is still always the risk you may not succeed, you are the master of your own destiny. So, the first knowledge I want you to work on, is knowing whether you want to get another job or if you want to work for yourself and start your own business. What do you think?"

"I just lost two jobs in 2 weeks and I felt I had no control about what happened to me," says Jean, "I believe I would rather be my own boss. I'm a self-starter and I believe I have some great training and ideas, but I don't know the first thing about running a business or how that would affect my personal life. Can you help me with your experience?"

"I sure can!" says The Guide with a big smile, "let's start by thinking about what knowledge can help you understand how to find the right role for yourself and then we can work on the plan to achieve that knowledge. I believe when you know what you want to do and how you plan to do it you'll find you're building up your emotional strength!"

"I don't know," says Jean, "With Covid-19 the types of work I used to do are not readily available any more. They may be some day but I can't control that."

"That's true," said The Guide. "as we're figuring out what your plan is let's focus on 2 types of "Mental" knowledge. The first is what I call skills knowledge. That is what you know that enables you to play a certain role. Like your knowledge of physical therapy and the human body enables you to play roles like a physical therapist or personal trainer. You may still need more skills knowledge to be a licensed physical therapist but you have the foundation already. Then there is what I call emotional knowledge. This type knowledge can be many different things based on where you need to build up your emotional strength. For example right now you won't be able to overcome your anxiety about supporting yourself until you gain the knowledge of how you are going to secure your future. Things that can help with this are having very specific goals, and then creating specific plans on how you'll achieve them and measure your progress. Does that make sense?"

"It really makes so much sense to me," replied Jean, "I always have thought about the importance of having the skills type knowledge but I didn't realize I needed the emotional knowledge too!"

"I'm glad you understand this now," said The Guide, "Let's build on that. What I want you to do today, so we can review it tomorrow, is to write down how you'll feel when you've achieved success and accomplished your purpose. Then think about and write down what goals you believe you'll need to achieve to make you feel that way. Then think of some specific things you can do right away to start getting to your goal. Don't worry yet about making your goals and actions perfect. Just get us a good starting point for our talk tomorrow."

Jean thought this was a lot to think about and do with only one night. She wasn't sure she could do it, but she told The Guide she would try!

P K E

P	Physical
K	Knowledge
E	Emotional

CHAPTER 16, DAY 5 OF QUARANTINE

Jean learns how to build a plan for success.

The next day The Guide had some calls in the morning, so she and Jean couldn't meet till that afternoon. This worked out well since it gave Jean more time to work on her assignment. When they got together in the afternoon, it was overcast and a little cold out in the backyard. Spring in Richmond was arriving, and so the days often still got cold this time of year. Fortunately, both Jean and The Guide had the right clothes for the season!

The Guide asked Jean how her assignment went. Jean said writing down how she'd feel when she accomplished her life's goal was really tough, but she thought about the successes she had in school and with work, and she knew those accomplishments made her feel strong and proud. The Guide prodded a little and asked if any other feelings came to mind. Jean said she wasn't sure what to call it, but it's that feeling you get when you help someone, and you know you made a difference.

"Those are all great feelings to desire." said The Guide, "As you can tell by my role as The Guide, I feel helping others is very rewarding. When I see I enable someone to grow and succeed, I feel I've done a little bit to make our world better. Ultimately, I'm proud of them and I'm proud of myself too for the part I played in their success. Besides helping others what else makes you feel strong and proud?"

"I feel strongest when I know what to do and then I see my plans work out like when I build a training plan for one of my clients and then I see them get more fit and healthy over time as I work with them," said Jean.

"And have you helped a lot of people as their personal trainer?" asked The Guide.

"Over the years I've worked with over 100 people and many of them have told me I made a big difference in their life," replied Jean.

"That sounds like a role that you love," noted The Guide.

"It is," said Jean, "I just haven't ever been able to support myself with just doing personal training."

"Did you notice, Jean, that you focused not on avoiding your negative emotions but on building up your positive emotions when you thought about how you've helped so many people?" said The Guide, "That is a critical learning for you. While you can learn how to deal with negative emotions that sap your emotional strength it is at least as important to build up your knowledge of what provides you positive emotions! It is like with your physical strength. Avoiding being sick is important but just avoiding sickness doesn't make you strong. You have to consciously work at building your physical strength like you do with your workout routine. The same is true for your emotional strength as well."

"I get it," said Jean! "That really makes sense."

"Great!" said The Guide, "Those feelings of accomplishment are important emotions for me too. Let me tell you how I worked on feeling that way in my life. I think you'll see we have a lot in common!.

As I mentioned before, I was "laid off" from my job during the recession in 1981, and I changed careers and started working in real estate. I worked at a local real estate agency here in Richmond as an agent, and I loved my work. Since I was the new person on the team, I usually had to do a lot to help the other agents and some of the administrative work in the office. I didn't mind because that gave me some income until I took my real estate license test and was able to be a full agent myself. Once I had my license, I could take on new listings as well as sell homes myself. After I got my license, I was mainly assigned to sellers of less desirable homes or buyers who were considered high maintenance by my boss. I still made a living, but I felt I could do better even after a few years, but I couldn't convince him to let me have more of the most desirable properties. He said everyone had to move up the ranks this way, and it wasn't fair to the other agents for me to move up more quickly than they had even if I was being more successful. I believed ability should determine who got the best listings, not seniority, but I couldn't convince him to change.

That is when it hit me that I needed to run my own business for me to feel in control of my life, just like my parents had. I remembered how hard they worked, but I also remembered how happy they and our family were.

The next day while continuing to work as hard as ever at my job, I started to define my life goals and to build my plan to start my own business. Just documenting my goals and building the plan made me feel better about myself! As I was doing this exercise, I also realized that while I had started out thinking this was about my career, I realized my plan wasn't just a plan for a better job but for a better life. Like having a family and having a strong network of friends, many of my goals were things my career would support but wouldn't replace them. Needless to say, I developed my plan and succeeded in starting my own company. I used a technique called SPACE that I'll tell you about after quarantine.

"Thanks so much." said Jean, "Your story inspires me and I believe with your help I can make a plan and be a success too!"

Build your plan for success by focusing on your most important goals.

○ **Tools:**
- Imagine how you'll feel when you've accomplished your goal
- Build a life plan not just a career plan

○ **Positive Trigger Words**
- Positive Emotions
- Be your own Boss

CHAPTER 17, DAY 6 OF QUARANTINE

Jean learns how to overcome being surrounded by non-believers.

Jean spends time looking into what she wants to do with her life and career while also looking for roles she can take on now to support herself. While she doesn't have a solid plan yet, she thinks about her physical therapy degree and the things she learned in school. Maybe she can use some of those skills to build her plan. She follows up with some friends and people she has kept in touch with from school. While many of them tell her physical therapy jobs can be great, some of them also think she has been out of school too long; a lot has changed, and her resume won't stack up against the people who went right from school into the field. She starts working on updating her resume and sees what they mean. Before posting it, she decides to sleep on it.

The next morning she and The Guide are having their daily talk over coffee. Jean tells The Guide about her idea to use her degree to achieve her goals but that some of her friends make it sound impossible.

"I can relate to feeling surrounded by non-believers," The Guide says, "it is important not to let other people define what you can and cannot achieve. Having a strong network is important, and it is good to seek their advice when making big decisions, but it is up to you to decide how to use that advice, or not, as you develop your plans. As long as you are a believer in yourself, non-believers can't undermine your emotions. Something like what you are experiencing, Jean, happened to me when I was starting out.

Soon after I built my plan for starting my own real estate company and making it and myself a success, I had a similar experience. This was the 1980s, and many people didn't believe a woman could run a business as a man could. My friends at work and home all applauded my desire to go out on my own, but they also spent a lot of time telling me how much I didn't know about business or real estate. Sure, I could sell, they said, but how do you run a payroll, or pay your vendors. Some even told me that being successful in business would hurt my chances of having a family. I could hardly believe what I was hearing, and I was sure they wouldn't be saying that if I was a man.

I'd thought about all these things when building my plan, so I felt they were wrong, but it was still distressing to hear these negative comments!

Fortunately, one of my friends and colleagues was different. He said he believed in me, and he'd be happy to be my coach as I started my business. I was grateful to have had a coach who had already learned and been through many of the things I was going to face. In fact, it was through one of my talks with my coach that we came up with our catchphrase, "The Real Estate Guide."

As my business grew, I kept my coach but began expanding my friends and family network to include those who believed in me, and I found myself spending less time with those non-believers.

Without having planned it at all, I found my respect for my coach turned to love, and I realized that he made me feel good about myself as a person, not just as a business person. As you may have guessed, that coach became your Grandfather!"

"Well," said Jean, "I believe I have my coach, I mean Guide! I'll work on my network and sort them into believers and non-believers so I can still keep them all as friends but use the believers to help me with my plans."

"I believe you understand," said The Guide, "and you'll make those non-believers into believers someday just like I did! I'll see you tomorrow so we can continue working on your plan for success."

Thrive even when surrounded by Non-Believers

○ **Tools:**
- Get a coach
- Set your own goals
- Build a positive network

○ **Positive Trigger Words**
- Inner peace
- Define yourself, don't let others define you

CHAPTER 18, DAY 7 OF QUARANTINE

Jean learns how to manage Training Fatigue.

Jean now knows her success will be driven by her and not by how others think of her. She works all afternoon on learning about the job market for positions in the physical therapy field and looking at other sites like LinkedIn. Jean wants to be her own boss, but she believes working in the physical therapy field will help her get the real-world experience she will need for her own business. She also feels this work will help her refine her specific goals and definition of success. As she takes a break for dinner, Jean starts to feel like she has barely scratched the surface of her research; she could research this topic a long time and still not know all she needs to know. She has a virtual dinner with her family and tells them her thoughts. They're all supportive, and The Guide reminds her that knowledge is the key to success, so she should keep working on it. The Guide also tells Jean to remember to keep breaking what she needs to know down into smaller pieces so she can see her progress. Finally, The Guide reminds Jean that sometimes you have to think out of the box to get to your end goal, so take time to ask yourself if the path you are pursuing is the best way to get to the result you want. Being agile enough to change plans is important since we can never know everything that will happen in the future.

Jean hits the Internet again after dinner with the goal of understanding the physical therapy market and the opportunities and roles that are needed. She starts by learning about all the different roles in a physical therapy clinic. Then she breaks those roles down into their specific functions. By doing this, she realizes that many of the roles in a physical therapy clinic are the same as roles in other businesses. This makes her decide to broaden her research to include physical wellbeing, not just physical therapy, and break down what roles are needed in that business. Jean gets very specific on only roles she can do with her current skills as an entry point for her plan. Often, that first step is the hardest, so Jean wants to get started in a role where she can help people, support herself, and start moving down the path to achieving her goals. Sometime after midnight, she falls asleep in front of her PC.

The next morning Jean does her workout and grabs a quick breakfast of fruit and Greek yogurt. Then she heads down to the backyard to tell The Guide how she has progressed.

The Guide listens carefully, and when Jean is finished, she says she likes the fact that Jean has broadened the definition of roles she's seeking to include physical wellbeing, not just physical therapy. She also tells Jean her approach of focusing on roles she can do today is the right way to get started.

"I feel like there is so much work to do just to get started," says Jean.

"You're right, it is a lot of work!" says The Guide, "Let me add a little more work for you to think about though. Ask yourself if you are seeking a job or a role?"

"What do you mean?" asks Jean.

"Well," says The Guide, "a job implies working for someone like a big company or even a small business. If you're seeking a job, your goal may be smaller, like getting a paycheck or getting through your day. A role means you might be working for someone else too, but you also might work for yourself, and either have your own company or be an independent contractor. When you find a role you can play, something that transcends the specific project you're working on today, it builds a foundation for your future. If you want to be independent and start your own business, you're seeking two roles; one as the person with the skills needed to help people in the way you've chosen, like physical therapy, and one as a business owner, even if that business only has you as an employee to start with.

It's important to think through this because the steps to your overall goal will be different based on your answer. To achieve your goal and overcome training fatigue like you're feeling now, you must build a detailed plan and build in the measurements of success along the way so you can track your progress regularly. It's a lot like with your physical workouts. Do you have specific goals, and do you track your progress?"

"Of course I do," said Jean," I not only track how much I exercise but I also track my heart rate, and other measures to make sure I'm staying healthy. Seeing my stamina improve as I add to my routine makes me feel good so I stay motivated to keep up my exercise and diet."

"Exactly," says The Guide, "You already know how to get to a goal, now you just need to apply those same principles to your career and life goals and it will work just as well!"

"That makes so much sense," says Jean, "I have been doing jobs in the past, but I wasn't making them part of my overall plan. Now I need to focus on the roles I need to play to achieve my goals! Part of that tracking will certainly include tracking my financial success but that is just one piece of my overall plan. I can track my career and life goals just like I do my physical fitness goals. I'm going to work on the next few steps in my plan and my measures I'll use to track my success."

The Guide smiled and said, "Jean you are really making smart decisions. Keep it up and let's look over where things stand again tomorrow."

Manage Training Fatigue

○ **Tools:**
- Build a plan
- Map your progess
- Learn from others

○ **Positive Trigger Words**
- Keep your eye on the prize
- Celebrate small wins along the way

CHAPTER 19, DAY 8 OF QUARANTINE

Jean learns the dangers of Overconfidence.

Since Jean is meeting with The Guide in the afternoon, she spends the morning working on her goals and detailed plans. Jean defines her long-term goal to become a physical therapist and build a physical therapy company around her practice. Her mission is to help people live healthier lives. Her short-term goal is to get a paying role in the physical wellbeing industry, which will help her learn the business and make her financially independent.

Jean is starting to feel good about her plan and her goals. Now she starts working on specific steps to get to her short-term goal and the high-level outline about how she'll achieve her long-term goal. Just getting these goals into writing and getting the first short term actions defined makes her feel confident that she's on the right track. Jean is surprised when her phone alerts her that her meeting with The Guide is in 15 minutes. The day flew by! Now, it's time to show it all to The Guide and see what she thinks.

Jean is excited when she and The Guide meet that afternoon. She shows The Guide her plan and explains all the steps she thinks she'll need to take to find her short-term role, as well as her high-level outline for achieving her long-term goal of having a physical therapy business and helping people live well."

"This all looks great," says The Guide, "let me ask you a few questions about both your short-term and long-term plans. Keep in mind; I think you've done great work in a short amount of time! Have you thought about how hard it will be to get your first role in the physical wellbeing business with Covid-19 closing so many businesses? Many people in these businesses are now unemployed. It may take longer to get a job if those businesses restart slowly. How will you get a job in what could be a slow industry? I believe in you, but I also want to make sure you plan for the risks you'll encounter and define what you'll do if they materialize."

"I appreciate your belief in me," says Jean, "however, I'm not feeling near as confident as I did this morning based on the concerns you've raised. Are you saying I won't be able to achieve my goals?"

"Not at all!" said The Guide, "I firmly believe you will do great things! However, while it is great to be confident in yourself, it is also important to understand the risks and challenges you may encounter. Let me tell you a story about my real estate business and how I managed my overconfidence and kept on track to achieve my goals.

My timing for starting my real estate business was great, given the housing boom in the 1990s. This led me to be so confident that I grew the business very fast. As long as the clients kept coming in and kept having more money to put into their homes, everything was great. I also was enjoying my married life, and we started our family. Your mother and your uncles were doing well in school, and life was good. Then the stock market tech crash of 2000 came, and within a few months, business conditions changed dramatically. Richmond didn't have a large technology industry back then, but many of our clients had most of their investments in the stock market. When those stocks and mutual funds lost much of their value, many people felt they couldn't afford a home or move to a larger home. People put off their home purchases until they felt more confident financially. While I had planned for the risks I knew about in the real estate business, I learned that unknown risks like a stock market crash could impact you more than known risks. I had a business plan, but it assumed the continued growth we had enjoyed during the 1990s. I thought I had identified all my risks, but they were all things I had experience with, like mortgage rates or school districts declining. All of the known risks I had identified were valid, but because I didn't know about the stock market, I hadn't planned for the risk that occurred and its impact on the real estate market and my business. I had to build a new plan to get through the current crisis and make sure we could have consistently great performance even if other crises happened.

I worked with my whole team to focus on our relationships with our clients. We cut back everywhere we could, and we changed our roles so that we did more ourselves and relied less on expensive outside services. We built our business so that even at the reduced levels we were experiencing in 2000, we could thrive. When growth started up again, as it always does, we expanded, but we also re-invested enough of our profits to get us through a long downturn that might happen in the future. It was hard, but we got through it, and I learned a valuable lesson, which is that even when you are winning, you can't let yourself be complacent."

"Keep your current action plans and goals." said The Guide, "but now add to them the risks and issues you can envision, and identify what actions you'll take to work through them. Then don't try to identify any specific unknown risk that could occur because by their nature, these are unknowable, but think of things that can make your plan more secure no matter what happens."

"I think I understand," said Jean, "I'm thinking that because the physical wellbeing business may be slow today I'll need to be able to start my role on my own timetable. I may have to start as just me doing personal training or classes from home to save money for example."

"I see you now know what I meant," said The Guide, "Go ahead and brainstorm more ideas like that for both your short-term and long-term goals. We can review them together after you feel you've identified risks and issues and possible solutions."

As Jean heads back to her basement apartment, she starts thinking about her plans and how to build in the things she will need if something out of her control happens.

Certainly, with Covid-19, she is getting a lesson about how life will change your plans on you in ways you could not have imagined!

Avoid Overconfidence

○ **Tools:**
- Stay focused on your plan even if you seem to be ahead
- Use data to make decisions

○ **Positive Trigger Words**
- Consistent performance
- Winning

CHAPTER 20, DAY 9 OF QUARANTINE

Jean learns how to avoid Post Event Failure.

Originally, Jean and The Guide were planning to meet in the morning, but The Guide texted Jean and asked her if they can postpone their meeting and talk after lunch today because The Guide has an emergency Zoom meeting with her friends.

"Of course," says Jean, "My calendar is pretty open these days."

This gives Jean more time to continue thinking about the challenges she'll face in finding the right role in the health and wellness industry. During her research, she finds out that physical therapy is an essential industry that hasn't completely shut down. Things have slowed down as people are putting off surgery or avoiding contact, but Jean does see some roles that people are looking for. While it will be a challenge, Jean feels confident that her personal training experience will help her find a role even if it isn't exactly what she would have thought of initially.

While the fact is that demand for physical wellness services is indeed down, Jean knows that in times of high stress like this, people need help focusing on their wellbeing more than ever. She also realizes that while people may need physical fitness services, they are probably doing less exercise due to the stress of the pandemic and of being isolated. As she continues to brainstorm more ideas, Jean likes the idea of starting to do some online classes and personal training. It's something she knows how to do remotely, and she has many former clients who will give her excellent references. Jean posts to her friends that she's available for classes and training and grabs a quick lunch before heading out to the backyard for her meeting with The Guide.

When Jean and The Guide meet that afternoon, Jean asks The Guide how her Zoom meeting went. The Guide says it was a tough meeting for her, but she believes she did some good. Curious, Jean asks what the meeting was about.

The Guide explains that she has kept the social network from her real estate days together. This group of about 12 – 16 people, depending on the day, are a mix of the people who bought her business, former customers who bought homes from her team, and some contractors she used to work with when doing real estate.

"They still look to me as The Guide," said The Guide, "I lead the group through discussions of topics they want to cover each week, and I help them with business and life challenges. Since Covid-19, we often talk about what we need to do to get through the next phase of this crisis. This week, we spent our time doing an after-action report on what's happening in the real estate and housing market, here in Richmond, right now.

People still need to buy or sell a home, but no one has done that during a pandemic before, or at least, not in the last 100 years. Our contractor friends are also figuring out how to work safely and still keep projects moving. Each of the people in our network sees a different aspect of the challenge the pandemic has brought us. While none of us has been through anything like this before, we're looking to accelerate our learning to deal with the pandemic through collaboration. This week, we took an example of a home for sale listing and a renovation project some of us had just done, and we had the team go through what had gone right and, more importantly, what hadn't gone great. My role as The Guide was to make sure we got to the details of what worked and what didn't, and that we learn to do better next time.

I also work to engage everyone in the discussion. It was a great meeting, and we learned a lot from each other's experiences that should make things go better next time around. Everyone, including me, left with a homework assignment about a post-event failure we recognized and brainstormed solutions for. We'll work together next to see how our action plans worked!"

"Wow," said Jean, "You know this helps me think about my current situation. I'm seeking a role in the physical wellbeing business. While business has slowed down a lot people's need for help with their health and wellbeing has actually increased. I need to find a role I can do ASAP to keep on track with my short term financial goals while learning more about the business overall. I'm starting by thinking of roles I can do that let me start helping people with my PT background and my personal training experience while also keeping my family safe. I have some ideas, but I'd like your thoughts on what you think could work as well."

"I'll help you all I can," said The Guide, "Why don't we start by naming all the roles you think you're qualified for and then we can eliminate the ones that are missing one of your key criteria like achieving financial independence or learning how the physical wellness business works."

Jean and The Guide then spent the rest of the afternoon brainstorming on many possible roles for Jean. By the time they are done, they have listed about a dozen roles Jean could do today, and possible short-term action plans to obtain each role and the potential risks and issues that come with them. They narrow them down from there to just a handful that might be currently possible, and they also identify how to limit each option's risk of infection for the family. As they break for the day, Jean realizes that she's has another night of homework ahead as she refines her list and continues to refine her action plan.

Learn from Post-Event Failures

○ **Tools:**
- After-action report
- There is no rank among the team when doing the after action report
- Follow up plans

○ **Positive Trigger Words**
- You can learn more from your failures than from your successes
- Collaboration

CHAPTER 21, DAY 10 OF QUARANTINE

Jean finds out how to deal with In the Moment Challenges.

Jean has now narrowed down her short-term goals to something that not only provides financial independence but also helps her on the path to her long-term goal to develop a physical therapy company. She also now has a list of specific actions she can take immediately to achieve her goal. She's thinking ahead to once the pandemic is over, and she wants to have a role in physical therapy while pursuing the educational requirements she'll need to be a licensed physical therapist. Finding work at any non-Covid-19 related healthcare place will be tough right now, but from her brainstorming with The Guide, she feels she's on the right track.

Reading an article on her phone the other day, Jean saw that healthcare unemployment is way up and that 78% of the healthcare job losses in April 2020 were in ambulatory settings like a PT clinic. Gyms aren't doing any better either. Jean still firmly believes in her vision and her long-term plan, but she knows that taking that first step in this environment will be a big challenge. With these headlines on her mind, she heads to the backyard for her daily meeting with The Guide.

After asking about each other's days and how their friends and family are doing, Jean lays out her questions and concerns to The Guide. She reviews her long-term goal of starting her own physical therapy clinic and her short-term goal of getting a role in the physical wellbeing industry. Then Jean mentions the news about how the business environment for everything from clinics to gyms continues to deteriorate.

"Those statistics you mentioned about rising unemployment and business closures are what I call In The Moment Challenges," said The Guide, "You'll always face In The Moment Challenges along your path to your goals. You're doing the right things to prepare to meet these challenges with your detailed plans and action items. Let me tell you about some In The Moment Challenges I dealt with during my career.

I think of these types of Challenges as In The Moment challenges because no matter how good your goals and plans are, we all have to work through these. While our business was doing well in the early 2000s, we couldn't predict the Great Recession in 2008. People couldn't get mortgages, and home prices fell, forcing many people into bankruptcy. Unemployment never got as high as it is now, but it was higher than it had been for decades. As I mentioned before, we had grown our business carefully and reinvested where we could, so we could weather the storm. But we had our own In The Moment challenges. While sales of homes slowed to a trickle and prices dropped, we still had to pay the mortgages on our investment homes. Some of our tenants lost their jobs and couldn't pay their rent. We had to make some very hard decisions and sell some of our properties at depressed prices and renegotiate loans on others. Renegotiating with the banks was very difficult because they were hurting too. We had to explain to them how if they reduced our payments or even deferred our payments to the end of the loan instead of now, they would keep our loan and not have to write it off as a bad loan. Fortunately, we had credibility because we had done our homework, so we convinced them that it would be a win/win situation if they worked with us to keep both our businesses afloat. That crisis strained my team and our business almost to the breaking point, but we made it through by working together and using our collective knowledge and experience."

"I know I lived through all that," said Jean, "But being in high school I didn't really understand how tough that really was. Now talking with you I see how you used your expertise and network to take a tough situation and make it a win/win. I think I can apply some of that in-the-moment challenge thinking to my situation. I believe I'll keep doing my homework and start networking to get leads on the right role for me. I'll also see if I got any responses to my posting about Zoom fitness training and classes. You said you have a group you are still The Guide for. Do you think any of them might be willing to talk to me about my goals so I could get their ideas about how to get started?"

"I'll ask my group at our Zoom call next week," said The Guide, "Let's talk more so I make sure I give everyone the best idea of what you can do and what advice you're looking for. I'll also ask them if any of them need some personal help with their fitness. The stress of the pandemic is causing a lot of people to turn to baking and they may need some help working off those pounds!"

Prepare to Overcome In the Moment Challenges

○ **Tools:**

- Subject matter expertise
- Know the data and know the people

○ **Positive Trigger Words**

- Win / Win
- Great outcomes
- Faster results

CHAPTER 22, DAY 11 OF QUARANTINE

Jean learns how to overcome Betrayal.

While Jean is doing her morning workout, she thinks of how much has changed in her life in just the past two months. Besides the pandemic and its restrictions, she has also moved across the country from Northern California to Richmond, Virginia. She's become better connected with her family, although she's lost some connections with her friends in San Francisco. While Mrs. Chen's kicking her out felt like a betrayal overall, Jean feels it's worked out well for her because if she hadn't moved back to Richmond, she wouldn't have gotten to know her Grandmother, The Guide, so well. One of the decisions Jean needs to make as she embarks on her plan is where to live. Should she stay in Richmond, or move back to the San Francisco area? Or, someplace new altogether. It's not something she needs to decide right away, but it is something she feels the need to decide relatively soon so she can start making new connections.

When she meets with The Guide for their daily session, she tells her about her feeling of betrayal, and that she feels wrong for that feeling since things are going well.

"Have you ever had to deal with betrayal in your life?" asks Jean.

"Well," said The Guide, "I think it is important for all of us to build our network with people we trust so that when betrayal happens, you've got them to support you and to help validate your reaction to it. I had to deal with a big betrayal in my business and my personal life during the same time, and my friends and family helped me get through it,

As I mentioned, during the Great Recession, the bottom fell out of all of the financial markets, including the real estate market. As the recession got deeper, we found that many of our clients were at risk with their mortgages, and many others lost so much in their investments that they couldn't get a new home. Many people lost their jobs, and that vicious cycle continued for years. We did the right things and managed to save our business, but I didn't tell you about the two betrayals that made that even harder than it had to be.

As our sales fell, we always looked for ways to tighten our belts, so at one of our first post-financial crisis team meetings, I asked our business manager to open up all our financial accounts so the whole team could brainstorm and work together to make the best of things. As we drilled down, account after account, we found it hard to find supporting documentation for many transactions. This bothered me because if we didn't understand all of our expenses and revenue, we could miss something important. I called in a friend from my network, Jackie, who is an accountant and asked him to audit our books for us to find out exactly what we were spending and what our sources of revenue were, so we could figure out where to focus our efforts.

After three days of digging through our books, Jackie stopped by my office and asked if he could show me some things he'd found.

"Sure," I said, "just sit down." Jackie closed the door, which made me a little anxious. Then he opened up his laptop. He sat close enough to me so I could see his screen. Jackie then pointed to a number of transactions he had highlighted. All were for payments to various companies we used for things like landscaping, advertising, etc. Then Jackie paused, took a breath, and said, "Jean, I believe your business manager is stealing from you. Not millions of dollars, but thousands of dollars a month adding up to over $50,000 last year." Jackie went on to explain how he believed the extra charges were getting covered up. He showed me an invoice from a supplier and then an invoice from another supplier for similar services. "By keeping the amount of each transaction fairly small and creating multiple fake "suppliers," I believe John, the business manager, has been funneling money to a company called Napping Cat," Jackie said. He then explained that when he researched who owned Napping Cat, it turned out to be John and his wife, and when Jackie checked these suspicious suppliers, they all were owned by Napping Cat! I was shocked and stunned. I'd never had someone on my team betray my trust like this before.

Of course, I confronted John with the evidence, and he denied doing anything wrong. He said he saw all the agents making a lot of money with their commissions, and he thought he deserved something extra too."

"What did you do then?" asked Jean.

The Guide looked like even remembering this made her angry, but then she got control of herself and said,

"I fired him on the spot and walked him out of the office. Then I called a team meeting with the rest of the team to let them know John had left our company and I explained why. I also took the time to meet one on one with everyone over the next few days to let them know they had my complete faith and trust. We all pitched in and took on the work John had been doing and I think while the incident was awful, it really brought the rest of the team together and made me realize that on a highly functioning team you cannot afford even 1 bad apple! In a lot of ways I handled it a lot like you handled Mrs. Chen's betrayal and moved past the anger, mostly, and turned the situation into something as positive as possible."

"That's awful." said Jean. "But it sounds like you and your team made the best of it and survived the crisis. You mentioned a personal betrayal as well. What happened?"

"That's even harder to talk about," said The Guide. "As I mentioned, everyone at work had to take on the work our business manager had done to keep the business going. That included me. I worked many, many long hours for the next few years and often had to work weekends. All our children were out on their own by then so that left your Grandfather alone much of the time. While we talked about it and he said he understood, I could tell things weren't great between us but I didn't know what else I could do. About 2 years after we had fired John, your Grandfather told me he had decided he needed to reinvent himself, and focus on himself. Unless I left "The Home Market," he said he was leaving me. I was stunned! I thought we would be together forever and I suddenly realized I didn't know the man I was with any more. I told him it was an unfair choice to force on me and that if he felt he had to leave, he should leave. Of course there was a lot more to it than that but in the end we got a divorce and he moved to Arizona. I hope he found himself. It took me a long time to get over blaming myself for his betrayal; my friends and family came together and helped me get through it. While it took a while, even with the support of my friends and family, I know that his leaving wasn't my fault and that I'm happier now with the people I trust. That is the biggest lesson I have for you about betrayal. When someone betrays you, it's important for you to keep your heart open to trusting others. It's hard and it may take time but remember there is more good in people than bad, and you must seek out the good!"

"Mom and Dad never told us about what happened between you and Grandpa," says Jean tearing up, "I'm sad that you had to go through that, but I'm very glad you stayed with your family so I've gotten to be your Granddaughter!"

Coping with Betrayal

O **Tools:**

- Review past behavior objectively
- Validate your opinions with your network

O **Positive Trigger Words**

- The best teams have NO bad apples
- Trust
- Openness

CHAPTER 23, DAY 12 OF QUARANTINE

Jean learns how to conquer Self Doubt.

The next morning when Jean meets with The Guide, she opens up to her and lets her know that sometimes, it feels like finding the right role right now is a nearly impossible task. Many businesses are closed, and many people are out of work, so it feels like she could be living at home for a long time.

"How can I overcome a pandemic when so many other people cannot?" asks Jean.

The Guide gives Jean an air hug, smiles, and says, "I know how that feels."

"Yesterday when I told you about the problems we had at *The Home Guide,* I told you the story of what we did to handle the betrayal and get the business back on track but I didn't mention my self-doubts."

"You had self-doubts?" answers Jean also with a smile. "I don't believe it! You are always solid as a rock and so in control of your emotions."

The Guide nods and says, "It may seem that way to you, but let me tell you I felt very personally responsible for hiring John and for not providing enough oversight and transparency so that I or others on my team would know what he was doing. I doubted my judgment, not only of people but of how I ran my business.

And when my husband left me, I spent a lot of time wondering what I could have done better to save our marriage. I felt that I must not have been balancing my work and personal life if I let him feel he had to leave me to feel complete.

As I mentioned before, this was right in the middle of the Financial Crisis of 2008, so I felt that based on my mistakes, people on my team could lose their jobs, and their lives could be affected! I felt that if we still had the money in the business that had been stolen, we could keep more people on the team through the hard times.

I hope you can see how all that would really get to anyone, including me!"

Jean feels a little sheepish now that she realizes the emotional impact this had on The Guide, and that she brought up these hurtful emotions.

"I understand how that would have hit anyone hard," says Jean, "How did you get through it?"

"I did some soul searching and thought about how many people I've hired and helped create good lives for themselves and their families. I also talked to some good friends about my divorce and gained their perspective on it. They helped me see that my actions weren't the cause of our break-up; it was something in my husband that made him feel incomplete. All this helped me realize that, while I'd made some mistakes, I had also done many things right.

I worked through some different scenarios for our business about how to make it through the Great Recession. I took an inventory of my strengths and realized that my ability to build strong networks and create win/win scenarios for people was as strong as ever. I decided to save money by not replacing our business manager, and we spread his work out among myself and others on the team. This helped make up for the money we lost, plus it gave many of us a better understanding of how our business was run, and it provided us built-in transparency.

In my personal life, I used my newfound independence to reconnect with old friends, and through our local community, I was able to meet new people too. I made my life richer by expanding my relationships, and in the end, I feel stronger and more confident for it.

Overall, I overcame my self-doubt through a really deep and honest look at my strengths and weakness and by taking actions to motivate myself.

It is normal for anyone to have self-doubt from time to time. Everyone makes mistakes, and no plan is perfect, but if you focus on your strengths and remind yourself of all the things you've done right, you'll have the confidence to overcome these negative emotions.

While you're still building your plan and you have a lot to overcome, think of where you were 12 days ago versus where you are today.

Jean, you've shown me your strength of character and self-awareness.

You've defined short and long-term goals worthy of you, which will enable you to help others.

And you are following through on your plan even though the environment is challenging." answered The Guide.

"I believe you're right," said Jean, "I've done more self-assessment and planning in the last 12 days than I did in the previous 28 years. And I'm proud of what I'm doing and where I'm going. I will resolve not to let myself get caught up in self-doubt, and when doubt does arise, I'll remind myself of how strong I am and how far I've come!

I believe I'll achieve my goals if I keep focused on success."

"Don't sell your life short." said The Guide, "You couldn't have accomplished what you have in the last 12 days without being the person it took you the last 28 years to become! I'll see you tomorrow and we'll keep working on your emotional strength."

Conquer Self-Doubt

○ **Tools:**

- Focus on your strengths
- Practice
- Create a solid plan

○ **Positive Trigger Words**

- You are strong
- You know how to do this

CHAPTER 24, DAY 13 OF QUARANTINE

Where Jean shares her Emotional Growth.

Jean has been thinking about what The Guide said about self-doubt and working through different scenarios to overcome it while focusing on her strengths. This gives her an idea she wants to get The Guide's advice on.

"Good morning," says Jean, "Can I ask for your advice about something?"

"Of course," says The Guide, "What's on your mind?"

Jean begins, "I thought a lot about your story of self-doubt yesterday, and it made me look at my own strengths and think about finding the right role in a new light. That got me thinking of different scenarios that I could plan out using my strengths.

I think the plan that makes the most sense to me is for me to not take a job with someone else but to work for myself as a personal trainer. Online now, and then when things open up again, start a small gym.

I am a certified personal trainer, and I think creating a business around fitness and wellness will help people who are cooped up at home today via online training and classes. Later, when things open up, the gym will let me help more people and offer additional services."

"That sounds like a good plan," says The Guide, "When I decided to start my own company, I had some similar ideas. While I didn't mind working for someone else, I felt I could do more than my bosses had ever let me do. I believed I could help more people through my own ideas better than by following up on someone else's plans.

I like how you're using your strengths to build your business. Have you thought about how you'll get your online customers and where you'll want to locate once you open the gym?

Now that you've defined your career plan, I want you to do the same thing with your personal life. Define your goals, build your plan, and be ready for the bumps in the road that life will throw your way along the way."

Jean says, "I believe I can use my social media presence and network of friends to get customers initially. I've also talked to some people in your network, and they all seem to have lots of ideas and contacts that I can build on. By keeping expenses low (working from my home gym/apartment), I can start small and build up over time. I stay in touch with many of my friends from San Francisco, and they know I'm a certified personal trainer, so between that established network and the new network that I'll build in Richmond, I have a good base of people to help stay fit. Then as the business grows, I'll hire some more trainers and add classes and the gym.

While I'm doing all that, I'll start doing the same planning and goal setting for the rest of my life; I can use these same tools!"

"You've really thought this out," said The Guide." I'm very proud of your emotional growth and I know with your determination and confidence, you'll succeed in whatever you do!"

"Yes," said Jean, "The more I thought about it the less I wanted to go back to working for someone else and the more I wanted to be like you and build my own business. You've given me the confidence and the tools to be a success!"

More air hugs follow before Jean and The Guide head their separate ways for the rest of the day.

Share your Emotions with Others

○ **Tools:**

- Share your thoughts and feelings
- Understand what your network (friends, customers, team, family) needs from you

○ **Positive Trigger Words**

- Your people make you stronger
- Open yourself up to others

CHAPTER 25, DAY 14 OF QUARANTINE

Jean shows her Emotional Strength.

Jean is beaming when she gets to their favorite spot in the backyard the next morning.

"I already signed up two of my friends from my San Francisco network for personal training, and I got two follow up posts from your network here! Thank you again for sharing all your knowledge with me and for giving me the tools to understand my emotions, build a plan, and take action to build my Emotional Strength!" Jean exclaims.

"I am so very glad to help you," said The Guide (AKA Grandma) with tears of joy in her eyes, "I think you'll find working for yourself and building your own business is very rewarding. I know I have."

"Someday I know you'll be able to celebrate your success with your loved ones just like I did." continued The Guide.

"Just a few years ago, in 2017, I got a wonderful surprise. It was right after I had decided to retire and sell my business to some of my associates. I was going by the office to fill out some papers and start saying some goodbyes. Of course, I wasn't planning to lose touch with all my friends and colleagues, but I knew it would be different. As I walked into my office, my whole team, many customers and suppliers, and their families and friends popped out and yelled, "Surprise!"

It was a surprise retirement party for me with The *Home Guide* team, family, and friends, many of whom started as and were still customers. Over 200 or so people filled the office and the outdoor space next to it to overflowing. While that also made me cry with tears of joy, I was also filled with pride that I knew all these great people, and in one way or another, I had done all I could to help them all. After everyone showed me such great support, I needed to show them how much it meant to me!"

Jean, I believe, if you stick to your plans as I know you will, you'll get to feel that same feeling someday, and there is nothing like it!"

Recognizing Emotional Growth

○ **Tools:**
- Understand your knowledge and skills
- Document your positive emotions

○ **Positive Trigger Words**
- Inner strength
- Mental toughness
- Self confidence

CHAPTER 26 DAY 15, QUARANTINE IS OVER!

Jean and The Guide reflect on all they've accomplished in the last 2 weeks.

As Jean and The Guide meet again in the backyard, they rearrange the chairs so they can sit together and talk. They agree that this isn't the end of their relationship, but it is the beginning of the next part of their journey.

Of course, since quarantine is over, they give each other a big hug!

The Guide says, "I'm so proud of the way you have taken my lessons and applied them to your life in these most unusual and challenging times. When I look back at the Jean I met two weeks ago, and the confident and proud Jean I'm sitting with now, it fills me with joy."

Jean thanks her and says, "I wouldn't have been able to accomplish so much in just two weeks without your help and guidance. But it isn't the plan I created that I'm most proud of. It's my belief that I now have the knowledge and tools to maintain my Emotional Strength no matter what comes my way."

The Guide says, "That Emotional Strength was in you all the time. You just needed to know how to access it and how to reinforce it when you faced a challenge! While we'll continue to meet and talk, let me give you a little summary of what we talked about over the last 2 weeks. Use this to remind yourself of your Emotional Strength, and to give yourself some support when you're working through each part of your journey through life."

BUILDING AND MAINTAINING EMOTIONAL STRENGTH THROUGH PKE

Physical Knowledge Emotional

1) **Identify Your Emotions**

Tools: Honest self-assessment, peer review, active listening

Positive Trigger Words: Self-awareness, Emotional balance

2) **Build Your Plan for Success by Focusing on Your Most Important Goals**

Tools: Imagine how you'll feel when you've accomplished your goal, build a life plan not just a career plan

Positive Trigger Words: Positive emotions, be your own boss

3) **Thrive even when surrounded by non-believers**

Tools: Get a coach, set your own goals, build a positive network

Positive Trigger Words: Inner peace, define yourself, don't let others define you

4) Manage Training Fatigue

Tools: Build a Plan, Map your Progress, Learn from Others

Positive Trigger Words: Keep Your Eye on the Prize, Celebrate small wins along the way.

5) Avoid Overconfidence

Tools: Stay focused on your plan even if you seem ahead, use data to make decisions

Positive Trigger Words: Consistent performance, Winning

6) Learn from Post Event Failures

Tools: After action report, there is no rank among the team doing the after action report, follow up plans

Positive Trigger Words: You can learn more from your failures than from success

7) Prepare to Overcome in the Moment Challenges

Tools: Subject matter expertise, know the data and know the people

Positive Trigger Words: Win / Win, great outcomes, faster results

8) Coping With Betrayal

Tools: Review past behavior objectively, validate your opinions with your network

Positive Trigger Words: The best teams have NO bad apples

9) Conquer Self-Doubt

Tools: Focus on your strengths, practice, create a solid plan

Positive Trigger Words: You are strong, you know how to do this

10) Express Your Emotions to Others

Tools: Share your thoughts and feelings, understand what your network (friends, customers, teams, family) needs from you emotionally

Positive Trigger Words: Person of character, open, good listener

11) Recognizing Emotional Growth

Tools: Understand your knowledge and skills, document your positive emotions

Positive Trigger Words: Inner strength, mental toughness, self confidence

CHAPTER 27

12 months after quarantine.

It's a bittersweet day for Jean. She's learned much from The Guide, and can hardly imagine not having her nearby whenever she needs her, but she's moving out today. Jean has been building up her client base in her personal training business online since quarantine, and now she is doing a virtual opening for her business through a YouTube video series and blog. She's moved into an apartment in the Fan district of Richmond, and she has a studio set up for her online classes. Besides personal training, she has added other wellness coaching services. Jean also applied for the Doctor of Physical Therapy program at the University of Virginia. She was just accepted and will start that program online next year when she is a full Virginia resident.

Jean knows that The Guide will be with her, but she also has confidence that she can handle the new challenges that come her way as she continues her journey as an entrepreneur.

EPILOGUE

5 years later

Jean and The Guide are having lunch together in The Fan district of Richmond. Jean shows The Guide the business plan she's getting ready to present to her new investors. She also shows The Guide pictures of her new boyfriend, Josh, on her phone.

"I really love him," says Jean, "We're very happy together, and we both love living in Richmond and enjoying all our friends together. I'm planning to bring Josh over to Mom and Dad's for dinner this weekend. Maybe you can come too?"

I've also been growing my gym while I'm completing my Doctor of Physical Therapy degree online. Now I'm ready to graduate and expand the gym and personal training business into a Physical Therapy practice. It's a big step, but I've planned things out well and developed my own network both at school and through the gym, so I know that with hard work and everyone's support, I'll be successful!

I'm looking forward to taking this next big step!"

The Guide smiles, gives Jean a big hug, and says, "That sounds great Jean and I'd love to go to dinner and meet your new man. I'll always be here for you as you continue on your Journey."

McCarley International Guiding Principles

The Guiding Principles below are not only those values that we now hold most important, but those that helped us get to where we are today. They have been the degrees of our professional compasses, directing our short-term decisions, defining our long-term path, and always reminding us where we have been and where we are going.

Do As Much Good For As Many People As Possible.

Our commitment to others will be demonstrated through our choice of actions and our choice of words.

Bring Value To Every Situation.

Be helpful all the time. Ask yourself what you can add to the situation. What can you make better?

Be Someone Who People Like To Do Business With.

Be fair, courteous, respectful and polite.

Help The Best Idea Win.

Whether the source is a teammate or a client, embrace their better idea. Don't defend a weak position. Trust is earned. Be sure your judgment is trusted.

Think And Act For The Long-Term.

Prioritize long-term success over superficial short-term gains.

Grow.

Strive to be better every day. Aim for continuous growth in all three components of PKE.

Be Patient For Results.

Have urgency regarding the creation of feedback loops through Planning and Actions.

Embrace Failure.

Success is the ability to go from one failure to another with no loss of enthusiasm. We learn more from our failures than our successes.

Work Hard And Enjoy Your Work.

It may be hard work, but on the whole, it must be satisfying work.

Express Yourself And Listen For Understanding.

You may have the best idea, but no one will know unless you summon the bravery to express yourself – to speak up. You may not have the best idea, but you will not know unless you summon the courage to truly and openly listen.

Earn Trust.

Trust is two things – competence and ethics. Trust is earned. Your "word" should not be given without thought. Manage and persuade not by an emphasis on authority, but through an emphasis on competency, influence, education, logic, and inspiration. Embrace honesty and candor as a way of life. Insist on the highest ethical standards.

Be A Teacher And A Student All The Time.

Great teachers find multiple ways to reach a student. Taking different tracts and angles until the student understands. Be a student – all the time. Embrace the fact that no matter how much you know, you have much to learn. Enjoy the growth of learning. And know that everyone has something to teach. Know that even a fly can do something you can't.

Focus On Goals.

Be clear on the goal and follow the formula of SPACE. If the goal is important, stay on it. If the goal drops in importance, let it go.

When In Doubt, Do The Right Thing.

When in doubt, do the right thing. If still in doubt, be fair.

**For more about McCarley International
please visit our web site at:
McCarleyInternational.com**

www.ingramcontent.com/pod-product-compliance
Lightning Source LLC
Chambersburg PA
CBHW060943120626
46557CB00003B/1122